People Around Town

MEET THE VET

By Joyce Jeffries

Gareth Stevens
Publishing

Please visit our website, www.garethstevens.com. For a free color catalog of all our high-quality books, call toll free 1-800-542-2595 or fax 1-877-542-2596.

Library of Congress Cataloging-in-Publication Data

Jeffries, Joyce.
Meet the vet / by Joyce Jeffries.
  p. cm. — (People around town)
Includes index.
ISBN 978-1-4339-9388-6 (pbk.)
ISBN 978-1-4339-9389-3 (6-pack)
ISBN 978-1-4339-9387-9 (library binding)
1. Veterinarians—Juvenile literature. 2. Veterinary medicine—Juvenile literature. 3. Occupations—Juvenile literature. I. Jeffries, Joyce. II. Title.
SF756.J44 2013
636.089—dc23

First Edition

Published in 2014 by
Gareth Stevens Publishing
111 East 14th Street, Suite 349
New York, NY 10003

Copyright © 2014 Gareth Stevens Publishing

Editor: Ryan Nagelhout
Designer: Nicholas Domiano

Photo credits: Cover, p. 1 Comstock/Thinkstock.com; pp. 5, 11, 15, 24 (wing) iStockphoto/Thinkstock.com; p. 7 GK Hart/Vikki Hart/Taxi/Getty Images; pp. 9, 24 (medicine) pixshots/Shutterstock.com; p. 13 Maggie 1/Shutterstock.com; p. 17 Dean Golija/Thinkstock.com; p. 19 Monkey Business/Thinkstock.com; pp. 21, 24 John Wood Photography/Stock Image/Getty Images; p. 23 Hemera/Thinkstock.com.

Printed in the United States of America

CPSIA compliance information: Batch #CS13GS: For further information contact Gareth Stevens, New York, New York at 1-800-542-2595.

Contents

Vets help animals!

They are
animal doctors.

They can give pets
things to feel better.
This is called medicine.

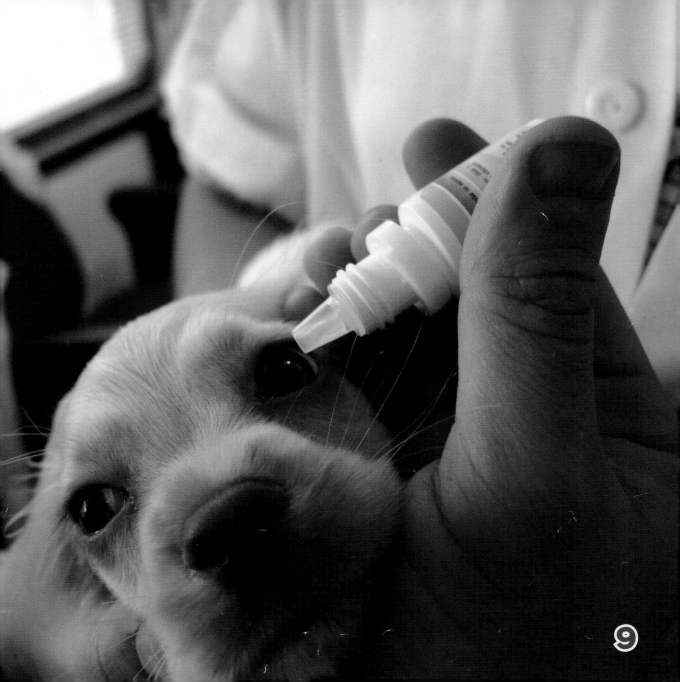

They fix a cat's paw.

They clean
a dog's teeth!

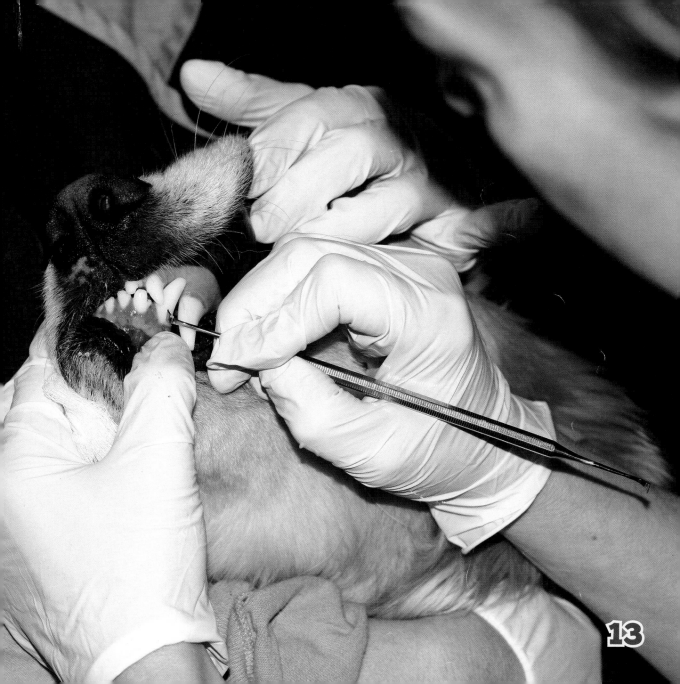

13

They set a bird's
broken wing.

Most vets work
in their own office.

They visit farms to help sick cows and sheep.

Some work with horses.
These are called
equine veterinarians.

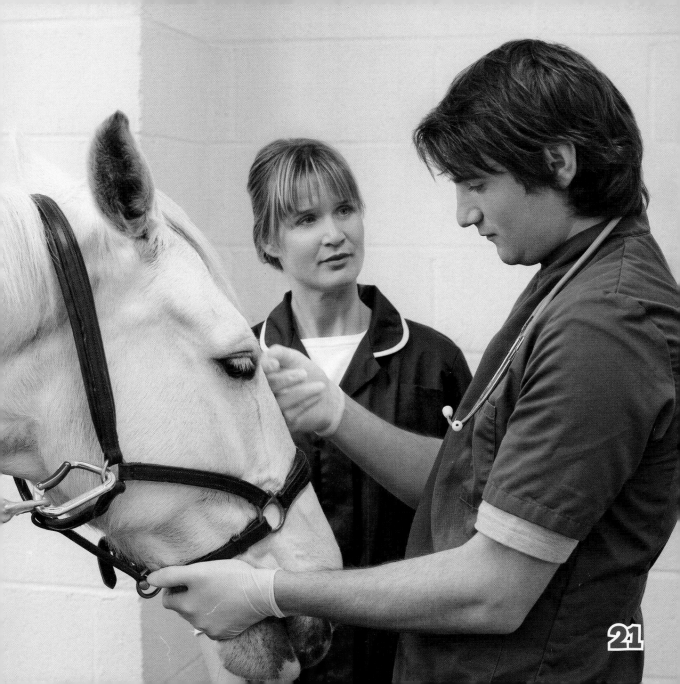

Others work at the zoo!
They help big cats
like lions and tigers.

Words to Know

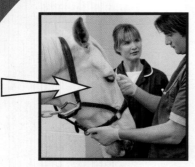
horse

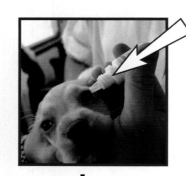
medicine

wing

Index

24